SPUNK

A SHORT STORY

By

ZORA NEALE HURSTON

INCLUDING THE
INTRODUCTORY ESSAY
*A Brief History of
the Harlem Renaissance*

First published in 1925

Read & Co.

CONTENTS

A BRIEF
HISTORY OF THE
HARLEM RENAISSANCE

The period of the Harlem Renaissance between the 1910s and the 1930s was a hotbed of African American artistic and cultural revival. Coined as "the New Negro Movement" by Alain Locke, it took place in the three square miles of Harlem, New York, in what became the centre of African American artistic opportunity. It was a time and a place that was prominent for Black creatives, becoming an influential microcosm of talent across the fields of art, literature, music, and more. The likes of Langston Hughes and Zora Neal Hurston, along with their contemporaries like James Weldon Johnson, Countee Cullen, Alice Dunbar Nelson, W.E.B. Du Bois, Nella Larson, Claude McKay, Jean Toomer, Anne Spencer and Angelina Weld Grimké were all prominent writers, artists and thinkers during the time. Each created work that would go on to establish a new African American identity within the late-modern era, from poetry to essays to novels, all rooted in the unique Black experience. Labelled "the Negro capital of the world" by one of its most prominent literary figures, James Weldon Johnson, the neighbourhood of Harlem was a catalyst for creative talent.

As a consequence of the Great Migration of African Americans from the southern states, Harlem became an area of prolific social and cultural change. The mass internal movement saw people travel north seeking higher-paid work and education opportunities and, most prominently, freedom from Jim Crow laws' oppression. The First World War had displaced many of the low-wage European labourers back to their homes, allowing jobs in the bigger cities to be filled by African Americans escaping the racial segregation and prolific lynchings in the American South. While a cultural revolution was also happening across the country in northern cities like Philadelphia and Chicago, the neighbourhood of Harlem in New York was its epicentre. The mounting industrialisation and opportunities brought about by the War drew rural people to the cities, searching for work. This resulted in growing communities of African Americans in places like Harlem, creating an environment that encouraged a new culture to thrive. A flux of Black-owned businesses brought more people to the neighbourhood making for a flourishing community of African Americans in the heart of New York City, eager to carve a new future as free people.

Many of the leading African American writers of the era lived and worked within Harlem during the 1920s. James Weldon Johnson was an American poet, writer, and civil rights activist who moved to the area after serving in the War, arriving at the zenith of the Harlem Renaissance. His work celebrated the power of Black culture. It was steeped in the realities of the African American experience, using a Black vernacular throughout his later works to tackle some of the broader socio-political issues surrounding racial prejudice. His poetic contemporary

Claude McKay was another central figure in the movement, shrouding his work's political angle under poetic gauze. His most famous poem, "If We Must Die", published in 1919, became a prominent statement against the wave of Black discrimination and lynchings that followed the end of the First World War. The poem spurred a new wave of political awareness, and is often seen as a precursor for the liberal work that would follow. His seminal 1922 poetry collection *Harlem Shadows* spotlighted the difficult lives of African Americans and showcased the revolutionary spirit of the time.

Encouraged by prolific writer and philosopher Alain Locke, a new wave of young artists utilised the changing societal landscape in the 1920s. They created uncompromising works in their depictions of Black life in an attempt to reclaim an authentic African American identity, one that rejected the degrading and often racist stereotypes attached to their culture. As a new awareness around African American identity was formed, civil rights groups like the National Association for the Advancement of Coloured

People (NAACP) were established, issuing journals that celebrated young writers tackling social and political problems. Journals like *The Crisis* and *Fire!!* became beacons of African American creativity and voice, enabling white publishing houses and readers more access to the rich diversity of Black arts.

By the mid-1920s, the American Jazz Age was in full swing. The music produced in Harlem by the likes of Louis Armstrong and Duke Ellington filled the clubs in the city, gaining fashionable status amongst white audiences. Iconic places like the Cotton Club and Small's Paradise were established to provide Black entertainment to white customers. Originating in New Orleans, Louisiana, through the enslaved African American communities, the jazz genre was a statement of freedom. It stood for freedom from oppression and white cultural sensibilities, eventually becoming the soundtrack to the hedonistic era, infusing all aspects of society from literature to fashion. Prolific poet Langston Hughes filled his work with the jazz music of his culture, infusing it with the rhythms of ragtime and blues to create a new literary art form - Jazz Poetry. Best known as the figurehead of the Harlem Renaissance, his work inspired that of James Weldon Johnson, whose poems were rich with the same musical rhythm.

The focus on the urban Black experience had shifted exterior perceptions of African Americans from lowly rural folk to one of cosmopolitan sophistication, which consequentially spurred a movement for political change and artistic freedom within their culture. This ever-developing form of a new Black identity created room for queer culture to appear. Unconventional lifestyles were welcomed in Harlem, with queer culture thriving in the blues scene. While it was still illegal to engage in homosexual acts, much of the culture lived underground in clubs and bars. Prominent figures of the time like Gertrude 'Ma' Rainey (later dubbed 'Mother of Blues') and author Zora Neal Hurston were romantically linked to other women. Rainey and her contemporary Gladys Bentley were known to cross-dress, hosting drag nights amongst the safe havens of Harlem. The movement actively challenged gender roles and race issues, embracing feminism and queer culture, placing it far ahead of America at the time.

The playwright and poet Angelina Weld Grimké paved the way for such freedoms with her early play *Rachel*. Considered the first show of the movement in 1916, Grimké created a work that attacked the patriarchy at its core. An entirely Black troop performed the three-act-drama, purposefully created for the civil rights group the NAACP. It was a rebuttal against the recently released film *The Birth of Nation* (1915), which glorified the Ku Klux Klan and portrayed a horrifically racist view of Black people and their role in the American Civil War. The play narrates the life of an African American family in the northern states after the Great Migration and disregards the common degrading caricatures found in theatre at the time. The titular character challenges the Black stereotype by exploring different reactions to the widespread racial discrimination felt at the time. Grimké subtly articulated her lesbianism within her works, with some of her later unpublished poems expressing the sexual suppression she felt throughout her life. *Rachel,* created by a queer Black female author, has come to represent the beginning of the movement, a forerunner for the ground breaking work that would go on to establish this era as one of the significant political and creative periods in African American history.

Following in her wake was Zora Neale Hurston. She became one of the most eminent female authors of the time, penning over fifty works, including novels, short stories, plays and essays, all portraying the racial struggles of African Americans in the early 1900s. Tackling contemporary issues in the Black community, her works were published in the prolific African American journal *Fire!!* established by herself, along with writers such as Wallace Henry Thurman, Countee Cullen, Langston Hughes and artists Aaron Douglass and Richard Bruce Nugent. Together, they explored many controversial issues within the Black community through the voices of younger authors, touching on topics such as homosexuality, promiscuity, prostitution and colour prejudice.

This prosperous time in Harlem ended abruptly with the Wall Street Crash of 1929, promptly followed by the Great Depression. While artists and writers continued to create work, the wave of opportunity was ceasing. However, their work was not in vain. The outstanding contribution to all creative fields laid the foundation for the Black Arts Movement of the 1960s. It brought around new awareness for Black art, one that was considered serious in the elite art world. Artists and writers continued dealing with issues like race and sexuality while exploring the everchanging African American experience. The new Black identity forged in the centre of the movement also caused a rippling effect regarding political justice. A product of the ongoing persecution of Black people across the country and the continued racial segregation laws, the newfound sense of African American independence felt in this period forced a new awareness of civil and political rights, consequently leading to race riots and the monumental Civil Rights Act of 1964.

While this was a pivotal time for African American culture, it was not without its critics.

The major cultural reawakening that secured a new and unique identity within the wider American society was brandished by some as an assimilation of dominant white culture rather than an authentically African-American one. Although the socio-political landscape of the time determined the boundaries in which Black people could create a life for themselves, they were criticised for utilising what small freedoms they had to find their voice. Even from the artist's perspective, debates were held about how far they could push the boundaries to avoid playing further into the general and often negative stereotype. Harlem Renaissance author W.E.B Du Bois coined the term "double consciousness" in his work, *The Souls of Black Folk* (1903), to represent the duality in identity that formed at the meeting point between Black and American culture. It articulated a way to understand the expression of the newly forged identity of African-American people, with a heightened awareness of its reception by those outside of it.

As labelled by Alain Locke, this "spiritual coming of age" saw African American artists and thinkers seize the moment of group expression and carve out a new identity for themselves at the beginning of the twentieth century. While the movement was not confined to Harlem, the district became well-known as the centre of Black creative talent. A prolific time in American cultural history, the prominent creatives of the Harlem Renaissance created a new world for the generations to follow, establishing a new Black identity and awareness of such in wider society through their often poignant and thought-provoking work.

SPUNK

I

A giant of a brown-skinned man sauntered up the one street of the Village and out into the palmetto thickets with a small pretty woman clinging lovingly to his arm.

"Looka theah, folkses!" cried Elijah Mosley, slapping his leg gleefully. "Theah they go, big as life an' brassy as tacks."

All the loungers in the store tried to walk to the door with an air of nonchalance but with small success.

"Now pee-eople!" Walter Thomas gasped. "Will you look at 'em!"

"But that's one thing Ah likes about Spunk Banks—he ain't skeered of nothin' on God's green footstool—nothin'! He rides that log down at saw-mill jus' like he struts 'round wid another man's wife—jus' don't give a kitty. When Tes' Miller got cut to giblets on that circle-saw, Spunk steps right up and starts ridin'. The rest of us was skeered to go near it."

A round-shouldered figure in overalls much too large, came nervously in the door and the talking ceased. The men looked at each other and winked.

"Gimme some soda-water. Sass'prilla Ah reckon," the newcomer ordered, and stood far down the counter near the open pickled pig-feet tub to drink it.

Elijah nudged Walter and turned with mock gravity to the new-comer.

"Say, Joe, how's everything up yo' way? How's yo' wife?"

Joe started and all but dropped the bottle he held in his hands. He swallowed several times painfully and his lips trembled.

"Aw 'Lige, you oughtn't to do nothin' like that," Walter grumbled. Elijah ignored him.

"She jus' passed heah a few minutes ago goin' theta way," with a wave of his hand in the direction of the woods.

Now Joe knew his wife had passed that way. He knew that the men lounging in the general store had seen her, moreover, he knew that the men knew he knew. He stood there silent for a long moment staring blankly, with his Adam's apple twitching nervously up and down his throat.

One could actually see the pain he was suffering, his eyes, his face, his hands and even the dejected slump of his shoulders. He set the bottle down upon the counter. He didn't bang it, just eased it out of his hand silently and fiddled with his suspender buckle.

"Well, Ah'm goin' after her to-day. Ah'm goin' an' fetch her back. Spunk's done gone too fur."

He reached deep down into his trouser pocket and drew out a hollow ground razor, large and shiny, and passed his moistened thumb back and forth over the edge.

"Talkin' like a man, Joe. Course that's yo' fambly affairs, but Ah like to see grit in anybody."

Joe Kanty laid down a nickel and stumbled out into the street.

Dusk crept in from the woods. Ike Clarke lit the swinging oil lamp that was almost immediately surrounded by candle-flies. The men laughed boisterously behind Joe's back as they watched him shamble woodward.

"You oughtn't to said whut you did to him, Lige—look how it worked him up," Walter chided.

"And Ah hope it did work him up. 'Tain't even decent for a man to take and take like he do."

"Spunk will sho' kill him."

"Aw, Ah doan't know. You never kin tell. He might turn him up an' spank him fur gettin' in the way, but Spunk wouldn't shoot no unarmed man. Dat razor he carried outa heah ain't gonna run Spunk down an' cut him, an' Joe ain't got the nerve to go up to Spunk with it knowing he totes that Army 45. He makes that break outa heah to bluff us. He's gonna hide that razor behind the first likely palmetto root an' sneak back home to bed. Don't tell me nothin' 'bout that rabbit-foot colored man. Didn't he meet Spunk an' Lena face to face one day las' week an' mumble sumthin' to Spunk 'bout lettin' his wife alone?"

"What did Spunk say?" Walter broke in—"Ah like him fine but 'tain't right the way he carries on wid Lena Kanty, jus' cause Joe's timid 'bout fightin'."

"You wrong theah, Walter. 'Tain't cause Joe's

timid at all, it's cause Spunk wants Lena. If Joe was a passle of wile cats Spunk would tackle the job just the same. He'd go after anything he wanted the same way. As Ah wuz sayin' a minute ago, he tole Joe right to his face that Lena was his. 'Call her,' he says to Joe. 'Call her and see if she'll come. A woman knows her boss an' she answers when he calls.' 'Lena, ain't I yo' husband?' Joe sorter whines out. Lena looked at him real disgusted but she don't answer and she don't move outa her tracks. Then Spunk reaches out an' takes hold of her arm an' says: 'Lena, youse mine. From now on Ah works for you an' fights for you an' Ah never wants you to look to nobody for a crumb of bread, a stitch of close or a shingle to go over yo' head, but me long as Ah live. Ah'll git the lumber foh owah house to-morrow. Go home an' git yo' things together! '

" 'Thass mah house,' Lena speaks up. 'Papa gimme that.'

"'Well,' says Spunk, 'doan give up whut's yours, but when youse inside don't forgit youse mine, an' let no other man git outa his place wid you!'

"Lena looked up at him with her eyes so full of

love that they wuz runnin' over, an' Spunk seen it an' Joe seen it too, and his lip started to tremblin' and his Adam's apple was galloping up and down his neck like a race horse. Ah bet he's wore out half a dozen Adam's apples since Spunk's been on the job with Lena. That's all he'll do. He'll be back heah after while swallowin' an' workin' his lips like he wants to say somethin' an' can't."

"But didn't he do nothin' to stop 'em?"

"Nope, not a frazzlin' thing—jus' stood there. Spunk took Lena's arm and walked off jus' like nothin' ain't happened and he stood there gazin' after them till they was outa sight. Now you know a woman don't want no man like that. I'm jus' waitin' to see whut he's goin' to say when he gits back."

II

—————

But Joe Kanty never came back, never. The men in the store heard the sharp report of a pistol somewhere distant in the palmetto thicket and soon Spunk came walking leisurely, with his big black Stetson set at the same rakish angle and Lena clinging to his arm, came walking right into the general store. Lena wept in a frightened manner.

"Well," Spunk announced calmly, "Joe come out there wid a meatax an' made me kill him."

He sent Lena home and led the men back to Joe—Joe crumpled and limp with his right hand still clutching his razor.

"See mah back? Mah cloes cut clear through. He sneaked up an' tried to kill me from the back, but Ah got him, an' got him good, first shot," Spunk said.

The men glared at Elijah, accusingly.

"Take him up an' plant him in 'Stoney lonesome,'" Spunk said in a careless voice. "Ah didn't wanna shoot him but he made me do it. He's a dirty coward, jumpin' on a man from behind."

Spunk turned on his heel and sauntered away to where he knew his love wept in fear for him and no man stopped him. At the general store later on, they all talked of locking him up until the sheriff should come from Orlando, but no one did anything but talk.

A clear case of self-defense, the trial was a short one, and Spunk walked out of the court house to freedom again. He could work again, ride the dangerous log-carriage that fed the singing, snarling, biting, circle-saw; he could stroll the soft dark lanes with his guitar. He was free to roam the woods again; he was free to return to Lena. He did all of these things.

III

"Whut you reckon, Walt?" Elijah asked one night later. "Spunk's gittin' ready to marry Lena!"

"Naw! Why, Joe ain't had time to git cold yit. Nohow Ah didn't figger Spunk was the marryin' kind."

"Well, he is," rejoined Elijah. "He done moved most of Lena's things—and her along wid 'em—over to the Bradley house. He's buying it. Jus' like Ah told yo' all right in heah the night Joe wuz kilt. Spunk's crazy 'bout Lena. He don't want folks to keep on talkin' 'bout her—thass reason he's rushin' so. Funny thing 'bout that bob-cat, wan't it?"

"What bob-cat, 'Lige? Ah ain't heered 'bout none."

"Ain't cher? Well, night befo' las' was the fust night Spunk an' Lena moved together an' jus' as they was goin' to bed, a big black bob-cat, black all over, you hear me, black, walked round and round that house and howled like forty, an' when Spunk got his gun an' went to the winder to shoot it he says it stood right still an' looked him in the eye, an' howled right at him. The thing got Spunk so nervoused up he couldn't shoot. But Spunk says twan't no bob-cat nohow. He says it was Joe done sneaked back from Hell! "

"Humph!" sniffed Walter, "he oughter be nervous after what he done. Ah reckon Joe come back to dare him to marry Lena, or to come out an' fight. Ah bet he'll be back time and agin, too. Know what Ah think? Joe wuz a braver man than Spunk."

There was a general shout of derision from the group.

"Thass a fact," went on Walter. "Lookit whut he done took a razor an' went out to fight a man he knowed toted a gun an' wuz a crack shot, too; 'nother thing Joe wuz skeered of Spunk, skeered plumb stiff! But he went jes' the same. It took him a long time to get his nerve up. 'Tain't nothin' for Spunk to fight when he ain't skeered of nothin'. Now, Joe's done come back to have it out wid the man that's got all he ever had. Y'll know Joe ain't never had nothin' nor wanted nothin' besides Lena. It musta been a h'ant cause ain' nobody never seen no black bob-cat."

"Nother thing," cut in one of the men, "Spunk wuz cussin' a blue streak to-day 'cause he 'lowed dat saw wuz wobblin'—almos' got 'im once. The machinist come, looked it over an' said it wuz alright. Spunk musta been leanin' t'wards it some. Den he claimed somebody pushed 'im but 'twant nobody close to 'im. Ah wuz glad when knockin' off time come. I'm skeered of dat man when he gits hot. He'd beat you full of button holes as quick as he's look etcher."

IV

The men gathered the next evening in a different mood, no laughter. No badinage this time.

"Look, 'Lige, you goin' to set up wid Spunk?"

"New, Ah reckon not, Walter. Tell yuh the truth, Ah'm a lil bit skittish. Spunk died too wicket—died cussin' he did. You know he thought he wuz done outa life."

"Good Lawd, who'd he think done it?"

"Joe."

"Joe Kanty? How come? "

"Walter, Ah b'leeve Ah will walk up theta way an' set. Lena would like it Ah reckon."

"But whut did he say, 'Lige?"

Elijah did not answer until they had left the lighted store and were strolling down the dark street.

"Ah wuz loadin' a wagon wid scantlin' right

near the saw when Spunk fell on the carriage but 'fore Ah could git to him the saw got him in the body—awful sight. Me an' Skint Miller got him off but it was too late. Anybody could see that. The fust thing he said wuz: 'He pushed me, 'Lige—the dirty hound pushed me in the back!'—He was spittin' blood at ev'ry breath. We laid him on the sawdust pile with his face to the East so's he could die easy. He heft mah hen' till the last, Walter, and said: 'It was Joe, 'Lige—the dirty sneak shoved me . . . he didn't dare come to mah face . . . but Ah'll git the son-of-a-wood louse soon's Ah get there an' make hell too hot for him. . . . Ah felt him shove me. . . .!' Thass how he died."

"If spirits kin fight, there's a powerful tussle goin' on somewhere ovah Jordan 'cause Ah b'leeve Joe's ready for Spunk an' ain't skeered any more yes, Ah b'leeve Joe pushed 'im mahself."

They had arrived at the house. Lena's lamentations were deep and loud. She had filled the room with magnolia blossoms that gave off a heavy sweet odor. The keepers of the wake tipped about whispering in frightened tones. Everyone in the village was there, even old Jeff Kanty, Joe's father, who a few hours before would have been afraid to come within ten feet of him, stood leering triumphantly down upon the fallen giant as if his fingers had been the teeth of steel that laid him low.

The cooling board consisted of three sixteen-inch boards on saw horses, a dingy sheet was his shroud.

The women ate heartily of the funeral baked meats and wondered who would be Lena's next. The men whispered coarse conjectures between guzzles of whiskey.